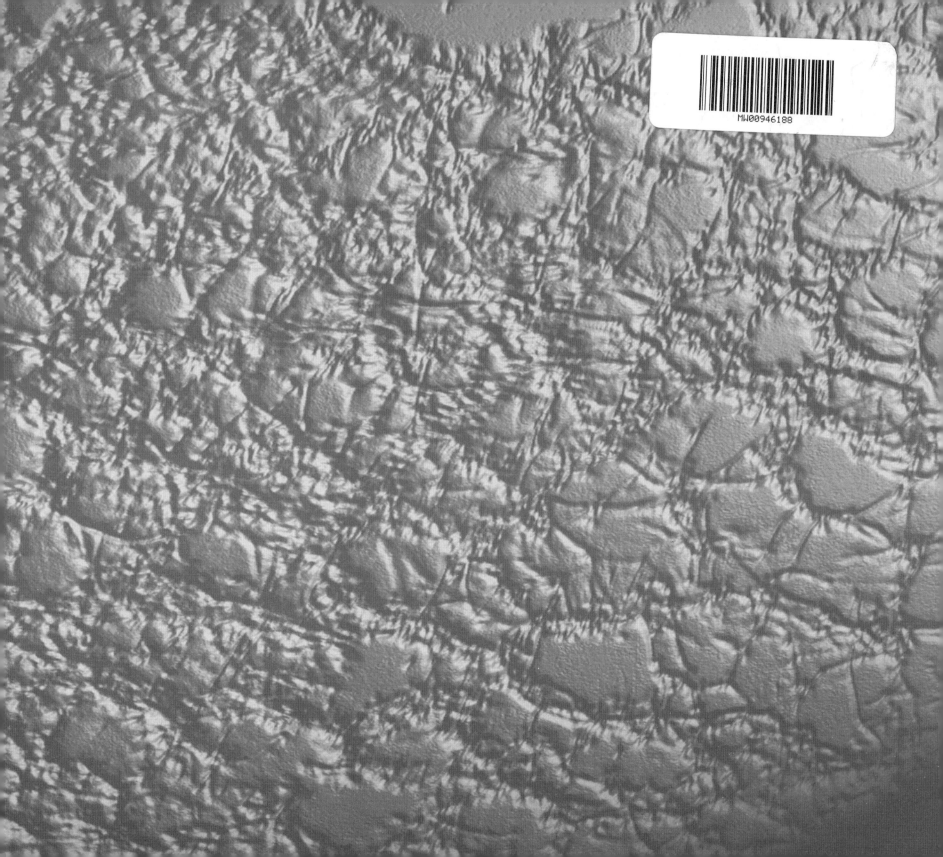

For My Family
I Love You All So Much

Time Soldiers®
Book # 1 REX

ISBN: 1-929945-18-3
Library of Congress Cataloging-in-Publication
Data Available

Previously published in 2000 as REX

Published by BiG GUY BOOKS, Inc.
7750 El Camino Real Suite F
Carlsbad, CA 92009 USA
Printed in Korea

Check out all the NEW STUFF at www.timesoldiers.com

Robert Gould's
REX
Book #1 in the TIME SOLDIERS® Series

Created and Photographed by Robert Gould
Digitally Illustrated by Eugene Epstein
Written by Robert Gould and Kathleen Duey

The woods smelled like rain. Squirrels and rabbits scattered, startled by the passing bikes.

"I can't wait!" Mikey yelled to his big brother. Rob grinned. He was excited too. In three days they were going camping and exploring with their best friends. They'd saved all summer for camouflage fatigues and packs...even rafts and slingshots.

Suddenly, Mikey braked, his bike skidding sideways. Rob swerved to miss him, trying to focus on the strange swirling light. This couldn't be real. A *dinosaur?* Rob flinched as it lifted its head to look at them.

"Run!" Rob screamed, stumbling backward. They raced for home.

Minutes later, Rob tried to describe the weird swirling trees and the dinosaur. Mom and Dad enjoyed the story...but they didn't believe it.

He finally gave up. "We're going hiking." Rob said. "All six of us." Mikey nodded. "OK, boys," Mom said. "Be home for lunch."

"Jon," Rob whispered into the phone. "Call Mariah. She can call Adam and Bernardo. Meet us at the club house and — "

"What happened?" Jon interrupted.

"Just bring the gear and wear your camouflage." Rob told him. "And hurry."

Rob hung up, giving Mikey the thumbs-up sign. They changed, then checked their equipment. Mikey got out their slingshots. "We might need these," he said.

Rob opened his bottom drawer and took out the old video camera Dad had given him. If nothing he said could convince his parents, getting the dinosaur on *videotape* certainly would.

Half an hour later the six friends stood staring at the swirling tunnel…and two dinosaurs.

"Apatosaurus," Mariah murmured.

"Can we go in there?" Jon whispered.

"We could explore it," Rob said. Adam nodded.

Mikey looked at Rob. "Let's do it!"

Rob and Jon led them forward.

Bernardo hesitated, then followed

8

Rob took a deep breath. The air was sweet with the smell of fresh lake water. The forest was so lush, so incredibly clean.

"Apatosaurus," Mariah repeated quietly. "They weighed 30 tons! Scientists argue about whether or not they lived in water."

"They seem to like wading." Rob said. His voice sounded strangely out of place here. It was so quiet he could hear the sound of his own heartbeat.

A rustling of wings overhead made them all whirl around.

Read the Time Soldiers
ADVENTURE JOURNALS at:

www.timesoldiers.com

MOTION SENSOR: LOCKED

10:27 A.M.

RECORDING: ● ◀| ■ |▶ ▶▶ BATTERY ▭

"What *is* that?" Bernardo asked.

Rob raised the video camera and framed the flying reptile, zooming in to get a good look. It was huge. He glanced at Bernardo. "Those wings must be 20 feet across."

"Quetzalcoatlus," Mariah told them.

"But that doesn't make any sense because — "

"Is it dangerous?" Rob asked.

The uncertain look on Mariah's face told him all he needed to know. "Head for the trees!" he shouted, pushing Mikey ahead of him as they all began to run.

MOTION SENSOR: LOCKED　　ZOOM: 10X

10:47AM

RECORDING: ● ◀Ⅰ ■ Ⅰ▶ ▶▶ BATTERY ▭

Rob counted helmets. Six. Everyone was safe...so far. The ground trembled, startling him. He turned, raising the video cam.

"Tyrannosaurus Rex," Mariah whispered. "Don't move."

Through the viewfinder, Rob focused on a leg as big as a tree trunk. His heart pounded...

It moved toward them. Adam flinched. "Run!"

Rob grabbed his arm. "No! Don't!!"

"Motion will attract it," Mariah said.

Bernardo was trembling. Jon put a reassuring arm around him. "It'll be OK," he said.

Adam closed his eyes. Mikey stood still as a rock, his fists tightly clenched.

The ground shuddered beneath the Tyrannosaur's massive weight as it moved through the brush. Then, abruptly, the dinosaur stopped. Rob heard branches breaking...then a dull tearing sound.

"It's feeding," Mariah whispered. "Its kill must be on the other side of those bushes."

Rob zoomed in for a better look.

"We can't stay this close," Adam said in a shaky voice, stepping back.

Rob turned to grab him, but Adam was already moving away. Bernardo jumped up to follow.

Then, in stunned silence, Rob watched as the T-Rex slowly lifted its huge head...

"Run!" Jon shouted, shoving at Rob.

Mariah yelled something, but her voice was lost in the thunder of the Tyrannosaur's roar...a sound that made Rob's teeth vibrate. Running was useless. "Climb!" He shouted. "Hide in the trees!"

Mikey found a low branch and started climbing.

Rob followed him, clutching the videocam tightly. Once he and his brother were on a sturdy limb he glanced back. Jon and Adam were in a tree across the clearing. Mariah and Bernardo were closer. They looked terrified.

The T-Rex was staring right at them.

MOTION SENSOR: OFF

ZOOM:10X

10:52AM

RECORDING: ● ◀| ■ |▶ ≫ BATTERY ▭

Rob turned the video cam back on and zoomed in. He could see the giant nostrils flare with each breath. Beyond the T-Rex he saw the kill, a small Triceratops. A darting motion caught Rob's eye. He lowered the camera. Two smaller dinosaurs were running through the forest, toward T-Rex's unguarded supper.

"Velociraptors..." Mariah shuddered.

"They're fast," Rob whispered as he pointed. Mikey nodded.

One of the scavengers was already tearing off a big chunk of meat...with needle sharp teeth. As it did, another horrendous roar exploded the air. T-Rex had seen the raptors,

ZOOM:10X

10:54:81

RECORDING: ◦ ◁ ■ ▷ ≫ BATTERY ▭

One of them looked up defiantly. The T-Rex attacked, its jaws closing around the raptor's neck. There was a sickening crunch...then an eerie silence.

The Tyrannosaur lifted its head, looking for the other raptor. Rob turned off the camera and scanned the bushes. Where *was* it?

"Rob, watch out!" In the silence, Jon's voice was startling.

"Shhh!" Rob hissed at him.

Then Mikey pointed downward, his face pale. Rob twisted around.

The second Velociraptor scratched wildly at the tree trunk, leaping up, snapping at his foot.

Rob jerked his leg upward, nearly losing his balance. The raptor jumped again...

A volley of sharp rocks spattered the tree trunk and the raptor's hide. Angered, it turned to face Mariah and Bernardo standing at the foot of their tree.

It took a leap toward them, then stopped as they reloaded and fired again. Rob heard the rocks hit hard. Shrieking, the raptor spun, then leapt away disappearing into the trees.

That was too close, Rob thought to himself. He lifted the video cam, zooming in to get a final shot of the raptor as it ran away.

Then he swung back around, still looking through the camera and...

ZOOM: MAX

10:58AM

RECORDING: ● ◀ ■ ▶ ▶▶ BATTERY ▭

Rob caught his breath.

"Oh no..." Mikey turned. "It sees us."

Rob nodded, lowering the camera.

The Tyrannosaurus wasn't as close as it looked through the zoom lens, but it was much too close for comfort, and it was staring at *them* now. There was only one thing they could do.

"Run for the river!" Rob shouted, scrambling downward. He made sure Mikey was running the right direction, then looked across the clearing. He could see the T-Rex moving through the trees.

Mariah was in the lead. Bernardo had slowed so Mikey could catch up. Jon was running hard, dodging trees and bushes. Rob and Adam followed close behind.

18

Mikey stumbled. Rob glanced back. The
T-Rex was getting closer. Suddenly, Jon
stopped and loaded a stone into his slingshot.

Rob held his breath as his best
friend took careful aim, drew back,
then released...

ZZZzzzzzzaaap! The stone struck hard, right between the Tyrannosaur's eyes. Startled, roaring in fury, the dinosaur charged, shaking its massive head.

Jon bolted, leaping fallen logs and diving behind a clump of bushes.

Confused by the mysterious pain, the T-Rex smashed into a huge tree and fell sideways. The ground shook violently.

"Can you see the river?" Jon shouted.

"This way!" Rob yelled.

At the top of the ridge, Rob saw the white foam of rushing water below. Jon jumped, skidding down the muddy bluff. Rob followed. Within seconds, everyone was sliding...

Jon was leaning, guiding his slide like a muddy snowboarder. Rob imitated him...and yelled at Mikey to use his balance. The wild slide was turning into fun. Rob glanced back at the bluff. There was no sign of the Tyrannosaurus.

"We made it!" Jon shouted as the slope leveled out beside the river. Everyone cheered.

"Oh no," Bernardo said.

Rob looked up, then quickly scrambled to his feet.

Staring hungrily at them was the biggest lizard he had ever seen...

"Inflate the rafts!" Rob yelled, searching for a rock. "Hurry!" Seconds later he heard air rushing into the valves. Focusing on the monster-sized lizard, he sighted on its face, then changed his mind. There were no trees here to stop an enraged attack.

He shifted his aim to the beard-like pouch under its jaw. Rob exhaled, then released and reloaded in one smooth motion. The lizard leapt back, startled by the sudden pain. Rob shot a second time...and once more the lizard moved backward.

"Get in!" Mariah was yelling."

"Come on!" Mikey shouted.

Rob backed up, watching the lizard. It flicked its tongue and turned away. Rob ran down the bank and jumped into the second raft.

Jon, Adam and Bernardo were already in the current, heading down-stream. The water was cold and swift. Rob paddled quickly, trying to catch up.

"We made it!" Mariah shouted over the roaring water.

Then she screamed...

Rob barely saw the giant rock through the whitewater mist. He dug his paddle in hard, steering the raft to the left. Mariah back paddled. They held their breath as the raft cleared the boulder by mere inches.

The two rafts shot downstream side by side.

"This is so cool," Jon grinned. "It's like we've been transported millions of years back in time."

"I just wish this place made sense," Mariah said as they entered quieter waters.

"We must have come through some sort of time portal," Rob said.

"Has to be," Jon agreed. "We're in prehistoric times."

Mariah frowned. "But some of these animals lived millions of years apart. I don't get it."

"Look," Adam pointed. "Triceratops."

"They belong here," Mariah said. "But the Apotasaurus doesn't and — "

"They look almost tame," Adam interrupted.

ZOOM: 5X

3:54 PM

RECORDING: ● ◀| ■ |▶ ▶▶ BATTERY ▭

"They're grazers," Mariah said as the raft rounded a bend in the river. "Not predators."

Mikey scooped up some clear water to drink. It was sweet and cold.

Bernardo pointed. "Apatosaurus?"

"Yeah," Mariah said. "More grazers...but from 77 million years *before* T-Rex."

Rob turned the videocam back on. He knew everyone would be amazed at these tapes when they got home. *If* they ever did.

"Maybe we should go back toward the portal..." Rob began, and then stopped. The others shook their heads. No one was ready to go near the Tyrannosaurus yet.

Learn more about Apatosaurus from **www.timesoldiers.com**

The forests thinned and the river narrowed as it passed into more arid country. They pulled the rafts ashore in a red sandstone canyon.

"No T-Rex here," Rob said. "No trees."

Mariah shrugged. "No one really knows where they lived."

"We'll tell 'em," Mikey joked. "Forests."

Everyone laughed. "We have to start home," Rob said quietly.

"How?" Bernardo asked.

"Follow the river back to the lake," Jon said.

Rob nodded. "And search for the portal."

"Hey guys!" Mikey called. "Some of those rocks down there sparkle like *gold!*"

"Look!" Adam yelled. "There's a passageway!"

"I'm hungry," Bernardo said quietly. No one answered and he sighed. "I want to go home."

"We all do," Adam said. He led the way. It was strange and beautiful at the same time.

As Mikey walked, he kept stopping to pick up rocks, putting them into his pockets.

Rob walked slowly, thinking. What were they going to do if they couldn't find the portal?

The Quetzalcoatlus they had seen at the waterfall was circling above them. "It's just curious," Mikey said.

Mariah nodded. "Like the Triceratops and the Apatosaurus. They've never seen anything like us before."

Learn more about flying reptiles at:

The sun was hot, and Rob was getting tired, when a sparkle in the rock made him blink. He climbed down and picked up a glittering stone.

"It's gold!" he whispered. He opened his hand to show Jon the shiny, yellow metallic rock.

"Gold!" Jon shouted. Everyone gathered to see.

"Look!" Bernardo said. "Here's another piece!"

Mikey grinned. "Are we going to be rich?"

"If I were rich, I'd buy the skateboard store," Rob said.

Jon grinned. "I'd buy a dirt bike and a go-cart!!"

Mariah laughed. "We could give money away to kids who didn't have any!"

They spread out, searching the rocks for more nuggets.

"We have to keep going," Rob reminded them

Mikey frowned. "I bet we could find a lot more gold if we could just stay a little longer..."

ZOOM: OFF

4:50 PM

RECORDING: ● ◀| ■ |▶ ▶▶   BATTERY

"Here," Rob said, handing Mikey the videocam. "Get a shot of me with this!"

Mikey was careful to hold the camera steady as he taped Rob with the gold against the amazing blue of the prehistoric sky.

"We better get going," Jon said.

Rob sighed. "Let's go guys." Adam looked up from the gravel he was sifting. Bernardo stood, dusting off his shorts. Mariah squinted into the sun as they started off.

4:57PM

RECORDING: ● ◀| ■ |▶ ▶▶ BATTERY ▭

Rob kept the camera on. The scenery changed as they walked, and the river widened again.

"What's that sound?" Bernardo asked.

Rob listened. He shook his head. "A waterfall? The *lake* had a waterfall."

Mikey found a way down the steep ridge... a great short cut through the house-sized boulders.

Everyone followed.

Read the Time Soldier's
ADVENTURE JOURNALS at:

ZOOM OFF

5:17PM

RECORDING: ● ◀| ■ |▷ ▷▷ BATTERY ▭

The waterfall was magnificent, but there was no river and no lake. The water bubbled up from underground springs, and then ran over the cliffs. Below, it roared into a crevasse that must have led to underground caverns and tunnels because the water simply disappeared.

Rob videotaped a huge flower Mariah and Mikey found. She was smiling. "I noticed one of these just inside the portal, when we first came through..."

"I hope we can find it," Rob said wistfully.

"Hey, you guys!" Jon shouted.

Rob stared, astonished. Jon was walking on *nothing!*

"It feels weird, Rob," he laughed. "Try it!"

Rob went next, making sure it wasn't dangerous. It was like wading through an anti-gravity puddle.

"Where's Adam?" Jon asked suddenly. Everyone stopped joking and turned to look around.

"I don't believe it," Bernardo said, pointing. "Look!"

"A Centrosaurus!" Mariah gasped. "A *baby* one!!"

"Is Adam doing what I *think* he's doing?" Mikey asked. "Hey, there's a baby longneck too!"

See Mariah's Fascinating Dinosaur Facts at: **www.timesoldiers.com**

Adam let the Centrosaurus sniff his hand. Then he climbed onto its back.

Everyone watched as Adam and the little dinosaur played, tearing back and forth.

Mikey tossed his pack to Rob, then ran toward the baby Apatosaurus.

Its mother looked at him closely. The baby was curious and friendly.

Mikey patted the little dinosaur. It lowered its head, and stared into Mikey's eyes. A moment later, he straddled its long neck. When it raised its head, he slid down onto its back.

It didn't notice his weight and followed its mother up the hill. Mikey rocked with the dinosaur's gait; its baggy skin felt cool against his legs.

On the ridge top, he looked down at a wide lake. In the dusk he saw a waterfall at the far end. A towering forest grew along the shoreline.

"Rob!" he shouted. "There's the lake!" He jumped down and ran toward his friends.

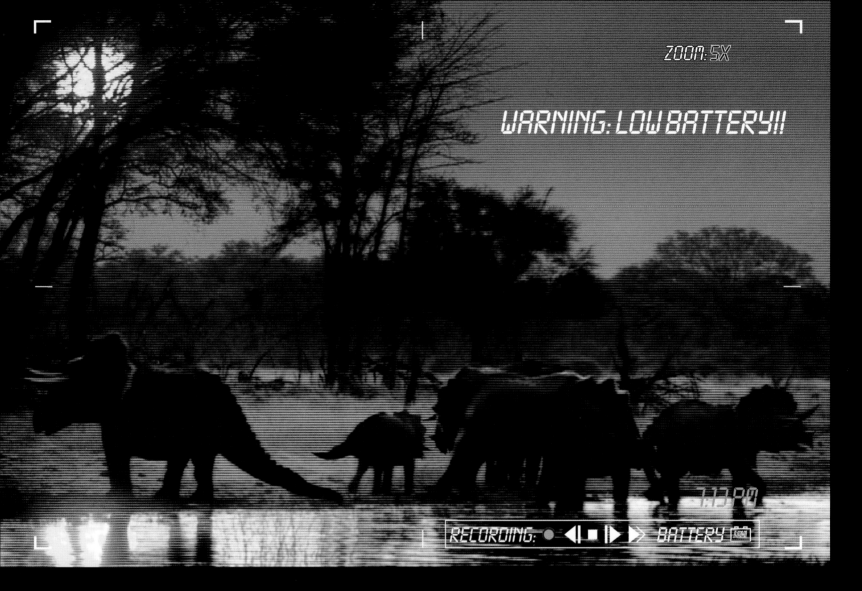

ZOOM: 5X

WARNING: LOW BATTERY!!

7:13 PM

RECORDING: ● ◀ ■ ▶ ≫ BATTERY 📷

"Can anyone see the portal?" Rob asked as they headed downhill.

"Not yet," Mariah answered. "But it has to be — "

"There!" Jon said. "I think..."

"I see it, too," Mikey said joyfully.

Rob raised the videocam and got a shot of the sunset-colored sparkle in the forest and the watering hole full of dinosaurs. The battery was almost dead. He zoomed in on the trees as the low battery warning sounded. A quick movement startled him...

RECORDING: ● ◀| ■ |▶ ▶▶ FAILURE

WARNING!!

The strange image in the viewfinder made Rob stumble backward. He lowered the camera and peered at the edge of the forest. But it was gone now.

"Rob? Are you all right?" Jon asked.

They took off their packs and threw them in first. It seemed safe. Rob clutched the videocam close to his chest and walked forward...into the portal. He felt a tingling prickle on his skin.

Coming out of the portal, he saw the woods,
their woods, in the morning sunlight.

Everything was calm and familiar.
It still smelled like rain.

"How can it *still be morning?*" Mikey asked.
No one answered.

"Let's get back to the club house," Rob said.
"We have to figure this out."

Jon nodded without saying anything.
They started off. Mariah glanced back.
She blinked, startled.

"Wait you guys! Look, it's...it's..."

"Look at what?" Adam asked.
Mariah blinked, then rubbed her eyes.
Rob frowned. "There's nothing there."
"Let's go," Mikey said.

Adam shrugged his pack higher on his shoulders. "Come on Mariah. You're just tired."

She glanced back once more, then followed the boys up the path.

"We were only gone an *hour?*" Rob kept repeating. It wasn't possible — but somehow, it was true.

"None of our parents will believe this," Jon said.

"The videocam," Rob said. He smiled. "We'll get them together tomorrow and show everyone the tape."

"Good idea," Mariah said.

"And not a single word to any of them until then," said Jon.

"And we never tell any other kids," Mikey added. "It's our secret."

Everyone promised.

It was a perfect plan.

But later, in the
silence of the night...

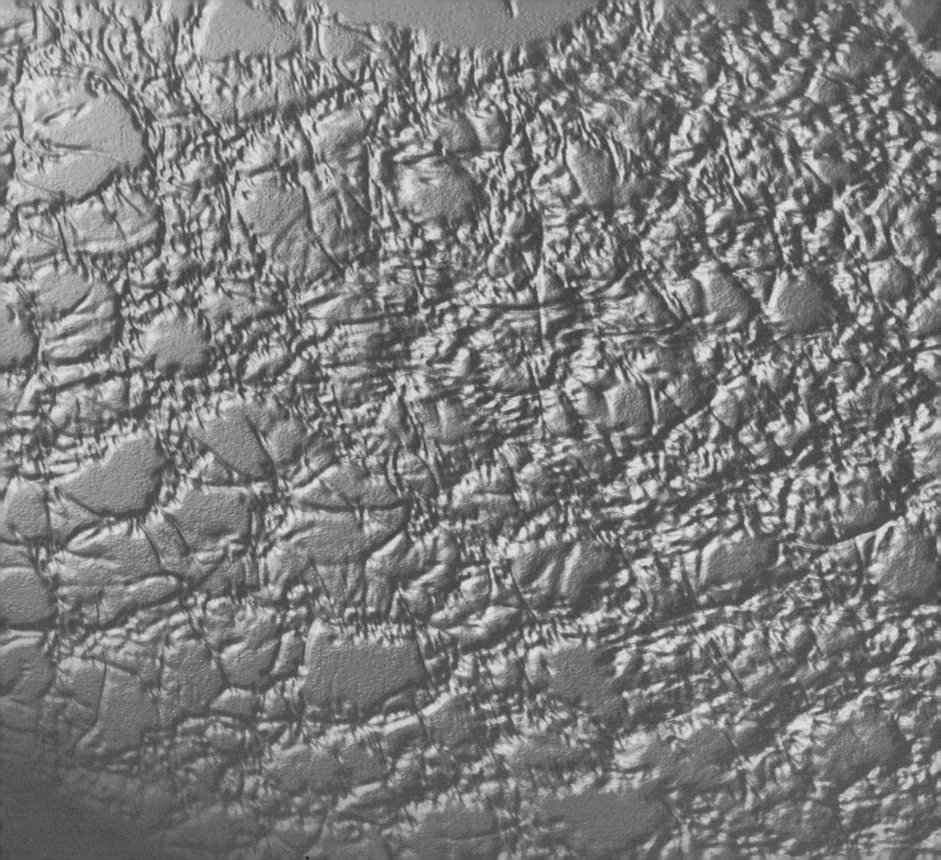

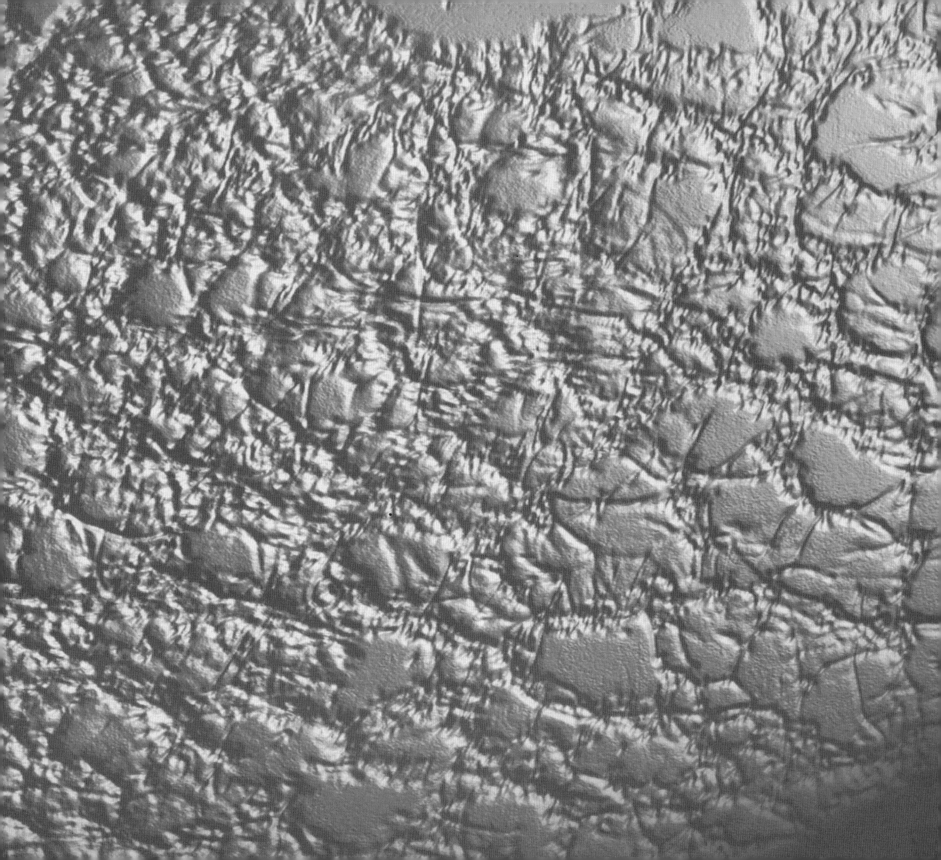

For My Family
I Love You All So Much

Time Soldiers®
Book #2 – REX2

ISBN: 1-929945-19-1
Library of Congress Cataloging-in-Publication
Data Available
Previously published in 2000 as REX 2
Printed in Korea

Published by BiG GUY BOOKS, Inc.
7750 El Camino Real Suite F
Carlsbad, CA 92009 USA

Check out all the NEW STUFF at www.timesoldiers.com

REX²

Book #2 in the TIME SOLDIERS Series

Created and Photographed by Robert Gould
Digitally Illustrated by Eugene Epstein
Written by Robert Gould and Kathleen Duey

The swirling light had led to quiet woods... a perfect place to dig a nest. But now, T-Rex could smell the small, dangerous invaders that had attacked the day before.

The egg could be in danger unless they were destroyed!

The scent-trail led to a hard, black path and the strangest place T-Rex had ever seen.

Jon was startled awake by the sound of heavy breathing.

He sat up in bed, hoping it was a dream. It wasn't.

Next door, Rob and Mikey awakened to a rattling of their windows.

The Tyrannosaurus stalked around the house. It was looking for a way to get in.

Across the street, Mariah grabbed the phone. "There's a Tyrannosaurus Rex--" she began.

"We handle *real* emergencies," the operator interrupted.

"It's true!" Mariah insisted. "Please, send help!"

Mariah didn't see the big black truck parked at the top of the hill. She didn't know that a tall man in a dark suit had intercepted her call.

She couldn't hear the harsh, hypersonic squeal of his top-secret equipment...

But T-Rex could…and it was painful.
The dinosaur ran to get away from
the terrible sound.

The neighbors were all fast asleep, except
one…the new kid in the neighborhood.

"We have to do something!" Rob said, dressing as fast as he could.

"Mikey, go get the video cam from the clubhouse. It's hanging on the wall."

A minute later, Mikey came back frowning. "Rob...the tape...it's gone."

Rob took the camera and flipped open the side panel. "Oh no!"

T-Rex was angry and confused. Why would this infuriating red animal *refuse* to get out of the way? A hard nudge had scared it and it began to call, a terrible wailing cry

that seemed endless. T-Rex placed one foot on its back and pressed down...hard.

The ear-splitting cry stopped.

Stepping around the defeated animal, T-Rex looked down the wide, black path and saw a huge lake. The water was moving. Curious, T-Rex saw more creatures in a strange hollow place as big as the biggest rocks in her valley. Strong smells came on the wind...water and salt, mixed with the scents of fire and scorching meat.

A sudden commotion in the parking lot startled T-Rex. There were more hard-skinned animals like the red one with the loud cry...rows of them...blue, yellow, white, brown and black.

Whirling to face them, Rex's tail smashed into the hollow place. The creatures trapped inside screamed and ran to escape. T-Rex turned to get away, and headed toward the moving water.

T-Rex waded in cautiously. Overhead, a noisy flying animal buzzed just out of reach.

Some of the small, dangerous creatures gathered on the shore.

They worried T-Rex. How many of them *were* there? Would they find the egg?

Everyone was geared up and ready to go. "What's the plan?" Adam asked.

Rob shrugged. "I'm not sure yet. First we have to find the Tyrannosaurus." He glanced back. An unfamiliar black truck was parked up the hill. It was huge...big enough to haul a T-Rex.

"Let's go!" Jon said. They flew downhill, cornering hard at the intersection.

The RG-TV news team was at the restaurant within minutes. Rod Luck and his camera crew linked to anchor woman Denise Fuller.

"We take you now to an incredible scene," she told her audience. "What appears to be a living dinosaur...a Tyrannosaurus Rex, is making its way north on the beach."

Jon got the first look. "It's headed for the oil storage tanks," he yelled.

He scowled, shaking his head. "Oh, no... an oil truck..."

Another noisy, flying animal circled overhead. T-Rex was puzzled. The tree trunks were the right shape, but they were smooth and white and smelled wrong. A big orange animal growled, then roared.

It sounded a deafening challenge as it moved closer. T-Rex attacked, ripping the enemy's skin. Strange, smelly blood sprayed out, then burst into flames. T-Rex was desperate to escape the searing heat.

Adam pulled out his binoculars. "The Tyrannosaurus wrecked the tanker truck," he said. "Wow! Now it's thrashing the whole area. Oh, man...there it goes!"

"Which way?" Jon demanded.

Adam lowered the binoculars. "Straight for the highway."

Rob pointed. "Okay. If we can get up the hill fast enough, maybe we can warn the

"How?" Jon asked.

Rob shook his head. "I don't know, but we have to try."

They pedaled hard. But it was too late...

Rex hated the wailing of the charging animals on the hard black path. It was impossible to fight them all.

There was no choice but to keep running.

On the hilltop, a field of flowers spread in every direction. It was quiet, until the buzzing throb of the flying animal came close, again.

Rex retreated, frantic to get away from it.

"Can you see it?" Rob asked Adam.

Adam focused the binoculars. "It's headed for the big construction site. Wow! You should see these guy's faces."

"Let's go!" Rob said, climbing back on his bike. "I know a short cut."

Rex stared. There were several of the big animals and two of the small, dangerous ones. Roaring, teeth bared, Rex lunged forward, then stopped abruptly.

There was a familiar scent in the air. Had it finally found the creatures it had come to destroy?

"It sees us," Rob shouted. "We have to create a diversion. That will give those guys time to get away!"

They scattered, pedaling in wild arcs,

kicking up fantails of dirt.

The T-Rex started after Jon, then switched to chasing Mikey. Mariah cut in close to distract it.

The equipment operators ran to safety, grateful for the kids' bravery.

"Maybe our rigs could hold it off!" one shouted.

Scrambling into their tractors, they started the engines...determined to help the kids.

The roaring of the hard-skinned animals was awful. Their breath was hot and

The small, dangerous creature inside it jumped free and ran. Rex turned

Rob stood on his pedals and turned in a tight circle, his back tire sliding. He controlled the skid, then shot forward, shouting to distract the dinosaur.

It spun around, knocking his bike sideways with a flick of its tail. Rob fell hard, sprawling on the dirt...

"Rob!" Mikey screamed.

But before any of them could move, broad wings swooped close to the rampaging T-Rex.

Desperate, Rob jumped, grabbing onto the Quetzalcoatlus as it rose, carrying him to safety.

He dropped to the ground on the ridge top. Looking back toward his astonished friends, he saw something very mysterious...

There was a long black truck pulling up...the same one that had been parked on their street. Two men in dark suits climbed out.

They carried the creepiest looking weapons Rob had ever seen. He ran toward Mikey and the others.

Without saying a word, the men lifted their strange weapons and fired at the raging Tyrannosaurus.

As the humming green light struck it, the T-Rex roared and began to stagger...

Rob sprinted downhill, then dove behind a giant dozer. "I saw that truck this morning!" he said, breathing hard. "On our street and..."

The ground shook as the T-Rex collapsed. Then, strangely, everything went silent.

The tractor engines had stopped running. The news helicopter had disappeared.

The men in dark suits lowered their weapons and stood looking at the fallen Tyrannosaurus.

Mikey stared at the truck. Whatever was inside it was connected to the time portal, Rex, and the missing video-tape! He was sure of it.

Mikey suddenly took off for the truck.

"Stop him, Jon!" Rob shouted. But it was too late.

Glancing around, Mikey climbed inside the truck. The metal floor was smooth, almost slick. He stepped forward cautiously. Computer screens glowed with columns of blinking numbers.

And there, placed neatly beside one of the monitors, was their videotape. *Yes!*

Enter Adam's "Men In Dark Suits" Contest at:

"Put that back." The voice was cold.

Mikey jerked around. One of the strange men was standing there. Mikey gripped the tape tightly. "You *stole* this."

"Just put it back." The man in the dark suit leaned forward to step up into the truck.

Mikey bolted, darting past him before he could react...

Mikey jumped as far as he could, landing hard, rolling to break his fall.

Scrambling to his feet, clutching the tape, he ran back towards Rob and Jon.

He thought he'd gotten away until...

Suddenly he felt an iron grip around his ankle. A second later he heard Rob's voice.

"Let my brother go!"

As Rob's boot slammed down, the grip released, and Mikey scrambled to his feet.

He ran faster than he ever had in his life. Rob was right beside him.

"Slingshots!" Rob shouted.

Slingshots at the ready, they faced the angry Tyrannosaurus...but it didn't come toward them.

Rob watched, puzzled, as Rex charged *away* from them, heading toward the woods.

Mariah pointed. "It's going back to the time portal!"

"Let's go!" Jon said.

They ran for their bikes.

Cutting corners, using every bike path and shortcut they knew, they managed to keep up with Rex...following it into the woods.

"Keep going!" Mikey yelled, swerving off the path. "I'll meet you there!"

He stopped, jumping off his bike to hide the videotape deep into the base of their secret tree. He knew it would be safe *here*.

Near the time portal,
Rob braked, astonished.
The T-Rex didn't even
glance at them. It didn't
look fierce any more. It
looked sad and scared.

"Look," Rob said, "An egg.
She... *she's* trying to move
her egg."

"So it was just --" Jon
began.

"-- protecting her baby,
Rob interrupted. "It's
a *mother* dinosaur."

Mikey and Adam
glanced at each other,
then lowered their
heads and stared at
the ground.

Mariah kicked at the dirt.

Bernardo wiped his eyes.

The kids stood in silence.

Rex pushed her egg gently into the portal. She looked back once, and roared...but it was an entirely different sound than they had ever heard her make before.

"Does she know we understand now?" Jon wondered aloud.

Rob glanced at him. "I hope so." Then he flinched. The men in dark suits were standing behind them. One of them was holding the videotape.

"Give that back," Rob demanded.

Mikey clenched his fists. "How'd you find it?"

The men remained silent. They simply looked at each other, turned around and walked toward the trees...

"Rob, look!" Adam shouted. "In the portal...who is *that?*"

Mikey turned to demand the videotape back...but the men in dark suits were nowhere to be seen.

"Look!" Rob shouted.

Jon whirled and stared at the closing portal. He blinked. A pirate? As he tried to focus, a sharp pain startled him. He pressed a hand against his forehead.

"Are you all right?" Rob asked.

Jon nodded. But the pain was weird, a giant headache behind his eyes.

The portal collapsed with a rumble, disappearing in a roil of dust.

Mikey glanced at Rob, then Jon. "They took our video-tape again. We can't prove anything."

"The portal will open again," Mariah said.

"It has to," Bernardo agreed.

"When?" Adam asked.

No one answered...because no one knew.

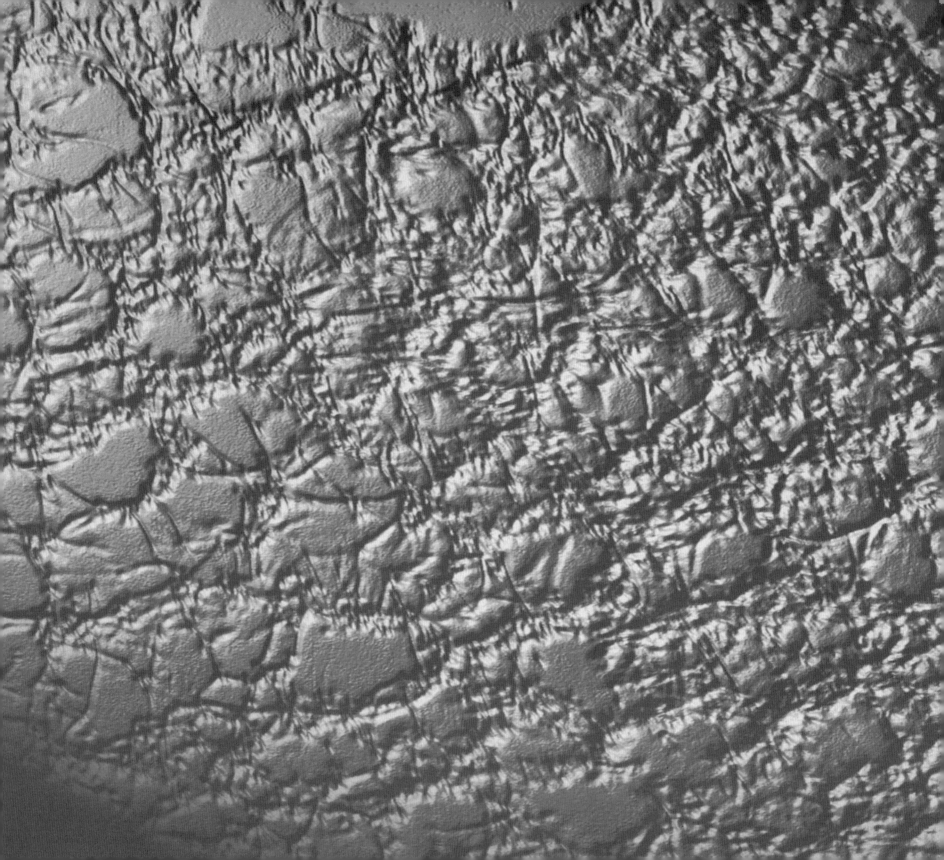

samurai

courage

Time Soldiers®
Book #6 SAMURAI

Text © 2006 Kathleen Duey
Photography © 2006 Robert Gould
Digital Illustrations © 2006 Eugene Epstein

Library of Congress Control Number: 2005935054

ISBN: 1-929945-62-0

Printed In China

Reading is more fun with
BiG GUY BOOKS Inc.®

www.bigguybooks.com

Published by BiG GUY BOOKS, Inc.
Carlsbad, CA, USA

Check out the cool stuff at www.bigguybooks.com

SAMURAI

Book # 6 in the TIME SOLDIERS® Series

By KATHLEEN DUEY

Created & Photographed by
ROBERT GOULD

Digital Illustration & 3D Special Effects by
EUGENE EPSTEIN

One rainy morning, six neighborhood kids find a time portal in the woods. Through swirling green light, they can see a living dinosaur! They can't convince their parents the portal exists, so they pack their camping gear and go through it, armed with a videocamera. They outrun Velociraptors, and outwit a T-Rex—and make it home with an incredible videotape.

Brian has made a tough decision. He's been accepted into special classes that will qualify him for a scholarship. Since he has to study so much, the Time Soldiers are looking for someone to replace him. They are all working to stay fit, research times and places they want to explore, and learn survival skills while they decide where to go next.

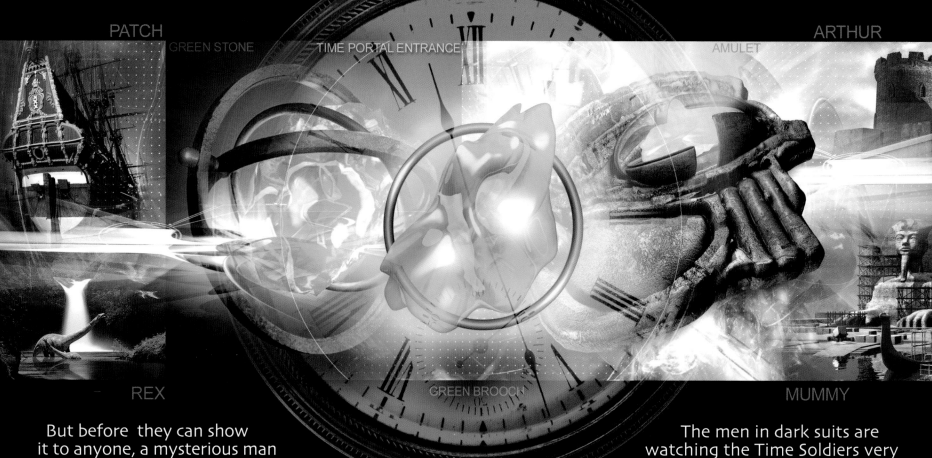

PATCH

GREEN STONE TIME PORTAL ENTRANCE

ARTHUR

AMULET

REX

GREEN BROOCH

MUMMY

But before they can show it to anyone, a mysterious man in a dark suit and sunglasses steals it.

The portal opens the very next day. Then nearly a year goes by before it transports them back in time again. Dinosaurs, pirates, knights, a boy pharaoh in ancient Egypt: With every adventure, the Time Soldiers learn more about history, about themselves, and about a timeless secret.

The men in dark suits are watching the Time Soldiers very closely. They know why the four oldest kids—Jon, Adam, Rob and Mariah—can't go through the portal anymore. They know about the strange green stones. And they know that time is running out… .

The library was quiet. "I can't decide," Luke was saying. "I want to go a hundred places." He noticed a girl sitting nearby and gestured. "She's here every time we come."

Mikey turned to look. The girl was lost in the book she was reading. "Maybe we should talk to her. We need someone smart."

"She's good at martial arts, too," Bernardo said. "I've seen her practicing at the dojo."

Luke leaned forward. "We should find out more about her."

Outside, Mikey introduced everyone. "My name's Nami," the girl said. "I've noticed you studying together. Is it a class project?"

Bernardo glanced at Mikey, then shook his head. "Not exactly. I've seen you at the dojo."

Nami nodded. "I want to do movie stunts when I grow up—I'll need to know martial arts."

Everyone liked Nami and they talked to her more each day. Finally, they decided to ask her to become a Time Soldier. She looked amazed—and excited.

"Could we go to Edo, the city that became Tokyo?" Nami asked, "I speak Japanese and I have samurai ancestors."

"Samurai?" Mikey asked. Bernardo and Luke smiled.

Two men in dark suits and mirrored sunglasses stared at the organic diode screen. The picture was perfect. "Should we get the stone now?" one asked.

The other frowned. "Why? They will find more pieces of it and—"

"Or they could lose it," the first man said.

"They won't," the second man said. "And we need at least—"

"I'm tired of waiting," his friend cut him off. "Is the new girl working out?"

The second man nodded. "And her father owns a film production company. No more costume problems. We should have thought of that."

"We're all getting better," Bernardo said after class. "Our research is nearly done. We're almost ready."

"The Samurai fascinate me," Nami said. "They were always trying to serve, to protect. But I'm a little afraid," she added. "You've done this before, but I can barely believe it's true."

"Everyone is a little scared," Mikey said, then he smiled. "We always stick together and we get home safe. And this time, you'll be able to translate for us."

Nami nodded. "I can't wait."

"These costumes are incredible!" Mikey said. "Are you sure your father won't mind?"

Nami smiled. "As long as we take care of everything, no one will even notice. I checked my father's production schedules. They won't need these for a year or more."

Luke nodded. "We had to borrow grave clothes in Egypt. We put them back, but it felt wrong to use them at all. This is going to be so much easier!"

Bernardo laughed. "In medieval England, we actually sewed our camp blankets into robes."

On a sunny Saturday morning, the Time Soldiers changed into their costumes and hiked into the woods. Bernardo held the amulet tightly. He focused his thoughts the way Brian had taught him and closed his eyes for a second.

When he opened them, the portal was waiting. They went in slowly, making sure Nami was all right. She held her breath—it was so strange to be hurtling through time.

When they came out of the swirling green light, they weren't in Edo. They were in a forest above the city. "That's Mount Fuji!" Nami said. "It's so beautiful."

Luke pointed. "I think I see a path that leads in the right direction."

They walked through the forest for hours before they came to a clearing. There was a dojo!

The Time Soldiers walked closer. "Look," Luke whispered, "a samurai teacher and his students!" Bernardo took a deep breath. "I managed to get us close to the city, but did I miss the time target?"

Mikey shook his head. "No, look at the clothes and the style of swords—we're in the era we studied, around 1700AD."

They all fell silent and watched the samurai working with his class.

The Time Soldiers hid and watched the classes until the sun was low in the sky. Then the samurai teacher started down the path, walking quickly, as though hours of training and teaching had not tired him at all.

"We should follow him," Mikey said. "He must know the best way into the city."

The Time Soldiers went just fast enough to glimpse the old man now and then. The plum blossoms made the air sweet. "It's so beautiful," Nami said. "I understand why the people here love nature so much."

An hour passed. Then two. "Did the teacher turn off somewhere?" Bernardo asked.

A moment later, the samurai leapt onto the path, his sword raised. Startled, Bernardo gripped the amulet as Nami began talking to the samurai in Japanese. Her voice was shaky, but the samurai

He spoke, then waited as Nami translated.
"I explained that we only followed him to find the city. He says if we camp with him, he'll show us the way in the morning."
"Taro No Yoshiie," the samurai said.
"That's his name," Nami said. "Bow in respect."

At sunset, the samurai made a campfire and shared his rice and meat. After they had eaten, he asked Nami where they lived. "Far from here," she answered in Japanese. "We came to learn about the samurai."

The old man raised his chin. "Samurai live in peace now. But when I was young, I was in many battles. One was in that clearing." He pointed. Nami translated.

"Would he tell us about it?" Bernardo whispered.

Nami spoke to the old man. He began to talk in a low voice.

The old man's voice was deep and strong. Nami translated.

"When I was young," he said, "I fought to defend my daimyo, my home and my ruler. I served him. I obeyed his orders. It was a hard life, but a proud one. He gave me a helmet for serving well."

"There was a rare stone set in it, the color of fine jade. I wore it the day I was wounded here—and lost it." He stopped, was silent a moment, then went on. "Our enemies fought well. We battled so long that the dust rose like sea mist around us."

Nami listened to what the samurai said, then, when he paused, she repeated it in English. Her eyes were closed. Bernardo watched the samurai's face as he spoke, describing the battle he had been in nearly fifty years before. Luke and Mikey were staring into the flames. Bernardo watched the old samurai's eyes fill with tears as he talked

about losing the helmet. He had been hurt—and he hadn't seen the thief—but someone had stolen the helmet. Another samurai? The old man shook his head. It seemed impossible.

The sunrise woke them all. The samurai led them to a tower, talking to Nami as they walked.

"This is so cool," Luke said as they stood, looking out over the battlefield.

"That's where he lost the helmet," Nami said, pointing.

After a moment, the samurai began to speak again. "He's talking about the battle now," Nami said quietly. "And he thanks us for listening to his old tales." She paused. "He says he would be honored to have us in his home."

As they followed the old man into Edo, he was talking to Nami. She kept turning back to translate. The samurai explained that the ancient city had begun as a single daimyo. Then other rulers had moved their families and farms closer to the sea. He was proud of his home. In Edo there were candles, he told them, that burned as bright as daylight, and swords that could cut a silk thread dropped upon the blade. Luke turned to Mikey and Bernardo. "We're walking with a real samurai!" They both nodded. It was incredible.

Taro No Yoshiie showed them the shogun's home. It stood like a castle on a hill. The shogun ruled over all the daimyos now, the samurai explained. "Wow," Luke thought to himself, staring at the ancient fortress, thinking about the long history of Edo and all the lives that had begun and ended here.

The old man smiled, then spoke. "He wants to take us through the city now," Nami translated, "before most people are awake." They all knew that the samurai was protecting them and they were grateful.

The samurai led them through shops and businesses. Then he followed one of the canals, walking toward the harbor so they could see the fishing boats. The Time Soldiers kept glancing at each other. It was strange to think that one day this city would be modern Tokyo, full of skyscrapers and cars. When the sun was low in the afternoon sky, the samurai finally led them back to his house.

The old man showed them his gardens. "Some of the bonsai trees are more than 200 years old," Nami said. "His ancestors cared for them."

The samurai's servants prepared food while he talked about the importance of honor. "He's teaching us like we're his students," Mikey whispered. Nami translated and the old man smiled.

After dinner, he showed them his swords and bows, then led them into the tea room. "He wants to honor us with a tea ceremony," Nami said. They all bowed to Taro No Yoshiie. They had read about this—the samurai was giving them an incredible gift.

Once it was dark and the old man had left them, they talked about trying to get his helmet back. They walked outside. Bernardo took the amulet out of his pocket. "I think I can get us to the exact place and time." Nami and Mikey nodded. Bernardo held the amulet tightly and summoned the portal.

In an instant, they were back on the battlefield—and fifty years back in time. The dark of night had vanished. It was a bright morning now and storm clouds were rolling in from the sea.

zone 12

83974593457BDF9OU000U493U49   8585091929 GSDH
8583423610   SG34RET348y459u-0845566NEEHM3345
2189349888OEO8YU9T0UUTO39OU0219U10U01U91290
4398IJR0PU0 CSFJO9U5095U095U0U330116

zone

spectrum analyzer

one 07

839744 94G7 IDF96
358134310 SG34
21893498880EO8Y
78398 JROPU0 CSF JO

858/7356843

zone

The two men were staring at their screens.
   One of them rubbed his forehead. "We never had adventures like this."
   The other man shrugged. "We didn't have time."
   There was silence as they both tried not to laugh at the pun. It was true. They had been on assignment and their orders had been very clear.

   "I wish we could just leave them alone," the first man said.
   The second man didn't bother to answer him. It was impossible and they both knew it. Their orders had not changed.

The sounds of the battle were close, too close. "This way!" Mikey shouted. They ran, then hid near the place the samurai had pointed out—the edge of the meadow where he had lost the helmet. The Time Soldiers were still and silent, watching the men fight. It was like they had fallen into an action movie, but this was real. The warriors were galloping toward their enemies. The archers drew back their bows to take aim... .

"Where is he?" Nami asked over the pounding of the hooves and the shouts of battle.

Then she pointed. "I see him! There he is!"

"He's been hit!" Mikey yelled.

They all gasped when the samurai slumped forward, then fell from his horse. The helmet rolled downhill. He reached for it, then fell back, closing his eyes. The ringing of swords got louder, mixed with cries of pain and the frantic whinnying of the horses.

"Stay low," Bernardo warned them as the battle surged closer.

"I wish we could tell him that he's going to live, that he'll have a long life," Nami said.

Luke stood up slowly. "I can get the helmet,"
"Be careful," Nami called from behind him as he
moved into the open.
Luke didn't look back. It took all his courage to
keep going—but he thought about the old man,
about honor, bravery, and protecting others.

He crawled toward the helmet, reaching out…

Just as Luke was about to touch the helmet, he glanced up and saw a man running toward him. A ninja? In the blink of an eye, the man grabbed the helmet and rolled to one side. Luke shouted, all his fear turning into anger. This was the man who had stolen the helmet so long ago.

The daimyo had given it to the samurai to honor his courage and loyalty—and this ninja had stolen it!

Luke stood and faced the man. The fire from one of the towers had spread—he could feel the heat of the flames. The ninja stared at him, then turned and ran, fading into the smoke. Luke sprinted back to his friends. They were all talking fast, trying to come up with a plan.

"We can't follow a ninja!" Nami was saying. "We'll never manage to keep up. We can't see where he goes and—"

"We can from up there," Luke shouted, pointing at the only tower still standing. An instant later they were all running up the hill.

"Can you see him?" Bernardo asked.

"No," Mikey said. "Wait. There he is, running down the path toward Edo."

Luke frowned. "I really wanted to give that helmet back to the samurai."

Bernardo hit the railing. "Me, too."

"Look," Mikey said. "The ninja's slowing down—he's turning into the forest."

"Spot a landmark," Bernardo said.

Mikey stared. "There's a crooked pine where he turned off. Let's go."

There was a second path, narrow and steep. They followed it downhill. Mikey and Bernardo silently climbed the steps of the little house to make sure the ninja was inside.

"Now what?" Nami whispered when they came back.

"I brought walkie-talkies," Luke said. "And Mikey has stink bombs."

Bernardo reached into the belt pack he wore beneath his kimono. "Two laser pointers, fully charged." Nami was staring at them.

Mikey turned. "We all bring something in case of an emergency. We usually have at least one."

Five minutes later, they had a plan and Mikey had climbed a tree. "Are the lasers bright enough?" he heard Luke ask.

"I think so," Bernardo said. "And it's getting darker."

"Stink bombs work day or night," Mikey joked.

Nami stared up at him. "Aren't you afraid?"

"Sure," he told her as he secured the walkie-talkie.

"We were afraid of the evil knight and the Egyptian temple guards, too." He climbed down. "If everything goes well, we'll be fifty years away from here in a few minutes."

Bernardo glanced at Nami. She looked a little scared, but she seemed steady—she was holding the walkie-talkie firmly in one hand. Good. They had known she was smart and brave and she was proving it. "Everybody ready?" he asked quietly. "I am," Nami said.

The ninja made a noise inside the little house and Luke jumped, startled. They were all tense. Mikey nodded sharply. "Let's go."

zone 12

zone

"unidentified radio transmitter"

(stinkbomb) updating the digital vocabulary

spectrum analyzer

digital rendering in process

zone

The men in dark suits were staring at the simulscreens. "I can't believe this," the first man said.

The second man was silent, then he exhaled. "They aren't bringing the stone back are they?"

The first man didn't answer. They both knew the truth. These kids were caught up in a thrilling adventure. Of course they would return the helmet and stone in it to the old man. They were good-hearted and honest—and they had absolutely no idea what was at stake.

The bright Edo candle lit the whole room. Nami and Bernardo got into position. He lifted his right hand to signal Luke and Mikey. Bernardo took a deep breath and turned the laser pointer on. The light was bright red, and the little cutout on the lens shaped the beam into a dragon. Bernardo angled the light so that the miniature

dragon appeared on the ninja's shoulder, flickered to the wall, then jumped back. The man turned, startled and confused. Bernardo shone the light at the far wall again. "It's working," he whispered to Nami.

Bernardo shifted his position. He shone the dragon-light against the window frame, then aimed it toward the door. The ninja turned to stare at it, then he took a step toward it. Bernardo nodded at Nami, then clicked the laser off. An instant later her voice, low and growling, came through the walkie-talkie Mikey had hung in the tree in front of the house. Nami sounded cold and stern as she pretended to be the dragon. She was challenging the ninja to a battle. Nami kept her voice low and fierce. "Come out and face us!" she said. "I dare you!"

The ninja stepped outside. Bernardo moved, turning on the second laser. He aimed the lights at the wooden porch beams. Nami knew the ninja had never seen a laser pointer and he had no idea what a walkie-talkie was. To him, the dragon's voice seemed real. "Can you catch us?" Nami snarled. "Do you dare to try?"

She signaled to Bernardo and he moved the light-dragons from the porch to tree trunks in front of the house.

For a long moment, the ninja followed the light-dragons with his eyes. Then, without warning, he leapt to the ground, his hands raised, ready to fight.

Bernardo lifted the lasers to keep the dragons out of reach as the ninja leapt and spun—then leapt again.

Bernardo kept the light-dragons flickering from tree to tree as the ninja spun and kicked, striking out, trying to defeat them.

Nami glanced up and saw Luke starting toward the window. Good. In a few seconds, he would have the helmet.

Luke had to break the window frame to get inside. He grabbed the helmet and climbed back out in seconds. Then he ran for the trees, careful to stay out of the ninja's line of sight. The helmet was heavy and he held it tightly to his chest as he circled back around.

The ninja was still trying to catch the light-dragon. Nami glanced at Bernardo and wrinkled her nose. He nodded. He could smell it, too. Mikey had set off the stinkbombs.

Bernardo moved the light-dragons lower, letting the ninja come closer to them. Then, at the last second, he moved the images to the next tree—and the next—leading the ninja farther from the house, farther from the path. Bernardo glanced back and saw his friends heading uphill. It was time to go. For a few seconds more, Bernardo

kept the light-dragons—and the ninja—moving. Then he jammed the laser pointer between two branches and aimed it higher than the ninja could reach—and ran to catch up with the others.

Bernardo held the amulet in his hands and forced himself to concentrate. They had to get back to the samurai, back to the safety of peaceful Edo. Behind them, the ninja spun around at the sound of their footsteps. "Here he comes!" Mikey warned.

Then the portal opened in front of them and they sprinted through it. Coming out into the darkness and silence of the samurai's garden, they all glanced back at the forest on the other side of the swirling green light.

"Can he follow us?" Nami shouted.

"Older kids can't go through without terrible pain," Mikey told her. "We're pretty sure adults can't do it at all."

Bernardo stared at the ninja shoving at the portal. "It almost looks like it's closing in order to stop him."

They all watched as the portal shrank and dimmed, then disappeared, keeping the ninja back in his own time.

"Taro No Yoshiie is going to be so happy to see this," Luke said, holding up the helmet.
"Look at the stone," Mikey said. "It looks like—"
"The stone in the amulet," Bernardo interrupted. "How can that be? Is it a coincidence?"

Luke wiped the dust of battle from the stone.

Suddenly, green light snaked between the stones. The helmet dragged Luke forward. He fought to hold on. Mikey helped him and they finally pulled it free, breaking the arc of light. "We need to do some research," Luke said. "Is there a green stone with magnetic properties?"

"One that can also open time portals?" Bernardo added, shaking his head. He put the amulet back in his pocket—the stone felt hot. "Let's go inside," Nami said.

Taro No Yoshiie's eyes went wide when he saw the helmet. "Tell him we wanted to thank him," Mikey said. "We wanted to show our respect and esteem." Nami translated as the samurai took the helmet. His eyes were full of happiness. A few minutes later, he left the room, then came back carrying a beautifully carved box.

"He says it is for us to keep our treasures in," Nami told the others.

The Time Soldiers bowed one last time and said goodbye, then walked a little ways into the woods to open the portal and go home.

"A box?" the first man asked. "Carved and lacquered and—oh no!" As he spoke, the image flickered, then went dark. "They aren't bringing the second stone back, and now they have a box that shields the first one?"

The second man typed quickly, then stood back to read the results. "It's lacquered with cinnabar— imported from China. The lacquer has mercury in it." He turned. "It's like the stone itself is planning all this. Now we'll have to follow them again."

48

"The dry cleaners mended the little tear in mine," Bernardo told Nami as they hung the kimonos back on the rack. "You can't even see it."

She smiled, then noticed Luke trying on cowboy hats. "That'd be cool," she said.

Bernardo nodded. "The Wild West."

Nami looked at them. "We could save up to go

to a riding school this summer. And we'll need to pick a time and place and—"

"Whoa," Luke said, and they all laughed.

To be continued

CREDITS

Time Soldiers
Luke - Isiah Jackson
Mikey - Michael Gould
Bernardo - Bernardo Kastlie
Nami - Kiana Pestonjee
Men in Dark Suits - Mark Flanagan, Kelly Shadburn
Young Samurai - Koji Kuninaga
Ninja - Sean Berry
Old Samurai - Master Richard Rabago
Martial Arts Teacher - Bruce Nguyen
Samurai Students - Katherine On
Kenneth Kim, Jae Lee
Cody Mau, Tiffany Le, Calvin Le
Samurai warrior - Master Ken Church

Special Guest Appearance - Briana Vigil

Kathleen Duey - Writer
Robert Gould - Creator/Photographer
Eugene Epstein - Digital Illustrator/Art Director/Story Board Artist
Mahsa Merat, Casting Director
Rakdy Khlok - Research and Costumes
Lara Gurin - Digital Composite Preparation
Jacob Dubizhansky - Digital Composite Preparation
Roman Gurinov - Image Masking
Carol Roland - Editing

Special thanks to:

Aya C. Ibarra - Japan Society of San Diego and Tijuana
Dave Tuites - Japan Society of San Diego Tijuana
Hiroko Johnson - San Diego State Curator, Historical Expert
Joyce Teague - Japanese American Historical Society of San Diego

Costuming and Props
Global Effects, Inc.
Kashu Sales International, Inc.
Aiya, Inc.
E-Bogu.com